My Birthday Party

An informational book

This edition first published in 2006 by
Sea-to-Sea Publications
1980 Lookout Drive
North Mankato
Minnesota 56003

Text © Barrie Wade 2004, 2006
Photographs © Franklin Watts 2004

Printed in China

Library of Congress Cataloging-in-Publication Data:

Wade, Barrie.
  My birthday party / by Barrie Wade.
    p. cm. — (Reading corner)
  Summary: Excited about her birthday, a young girl invites four friends to a special party.
  ISBN 1-59771-016-4
  [1. Birthdays—Fiction. 2. Parties—Fiction.] I. Title. II. Series.

PZ7.W1139My 2005
[E]—dc22

                                                    2004063729

9 8 7 6 5 4 3 2

Published by arrangement with the Watts Publishing Group Ltd, London

Series Editor: Jackie Hamley
Series Advisors: Linda Gambrell, Dr. Barrie Wade, Dr. Hilary Minns
Design: Peter Scoulding
Photographs: Chris Fairclough

The author and publisher would especially like to thank the
Hennessy family for giving their help and time so generously.

For Bethany—BW

My Birthday Party

Written by
Barrie Wade

Photographed by
Chris Fairclough

SEA-TO-SEA
Mankato Collingwood London

Barrie Wade

"I love sharing stories with children. I think children are brilliant writers."

Chris Fairclough

"I've been taking photos for books for almost 30 years and have visited 53 countries. Every day is different!"

Mom and Dad said I could have a party for my birthday.

First Danny helped me to write the invitations.

Then Dad helped me to deliver them.

Next we
made lots of
party food.

9

Naveena,
Isabel, Idel,
and Lily
came to
my party.

11

I gave them party hats.

They brought me presents.

We had
fun playing
party games.

15

After the games
we had cake
and ice cream.

We ate lots of
ice cream!

16

17

My birthday cake
had candles.

My friends sang
"Happy Birthday!"
while I blew the
candles out.

19

Everybody took
home some cake
and a balloon.

21

It's my birthday again in a year.

I'll write the invitations now!

Notes for parents and teachers

READING CORNER has been structured to provide maximum support for new readers. The stories may be used by adults for sharing with young children. Primarily, however, the stories are designed for newly independent readers, whether they are reading these books in bed at night, or in the reading corner at school or in the library.

Starting to read alone can be a daunting prospect. READING CORNER helps by providing visual support and repeating words and phrases, while making reading enjoyable. These books will develop confidence in the new reader, and encourage a love of reading that will last a lifetime!

If you are reading this book with a child, here are a few tips:

1. Make reading fun! Choose a time to read when you and the child are relaxed and have time to share the story.

2. Encourage children to reread the story, and to retell the story in their own words, using the illustrations to remind them what has happened.

3. Give praise! Remember that small mistakes need not always be corrected.

READING CORNER covers three grades of early reading ability, with three levels at each grade. Each level has a certain number of words per story, indicated by the number of bars on the spine of the book, to allow you to choose the right book for a young reader:

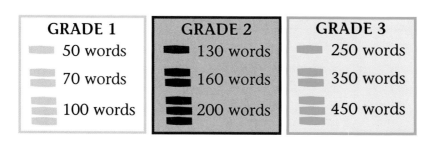

GRADE 1	GRADE 2	GRADE 3
50 words	130 words	250 words
70 words	160 words	350 words
100 words	200 words	450 words